She Who Sows

Courtesy Reaps

Friendship,

And She Who

Plants Kindness

Gathers Hearts

BEST FRIENDS

Loretta Krupinski

Hyperion Books for Children
New York

It so happens that certain sounds, sights, and smells of today bring back memories of yesterdays and my life on the river. When I hear rushing water I think of that year long ago on Salmon Creek. But it is when I see my old doll that I also remember my best friend Lily from my childhood. I wish the doll could tell me about the years she lived with Lily.

The doll was very special. She had real hair, blue eyes made of glass (not painted on), and lace trim on her dress. My ma and pa could never have bought me a doll like this. She was a gift from my Aunt Sophie.

"I hope you won't forget your Aunt Sophie when you and your ma and pa move out west," she told me. "You've been very gloomy about leaving Kansas, Charlotte, so perhaps this doll will ease your sadness."

I named the doll Mary, after my best friend. Pa took a job as a foreman for a cattle ranch. He said it would be a great adventure, and I would see sights that I had never seen before. I struggled with my feelings about moving. How could I be sad and glad at the same time?

On the train ride from Kansas to Idaho, I held Mary up to the window. For the first time in my life, I saw mountains. My adventure had begun.

Soon after moving to Salmon Creek, I discovered something even more special about my doll. My ma and I were sitting outside on the steps to our new home. I was cradling my doll so tightly her head fell off. I thought she was ruined forever.

"Don't cry, Charlotte. Look, it's not broken. The head just needs to be screwed back on." I hugged my ma, again cradling the doll in my arms, but this time gently——as if she really felt some pain from losing her head. Together the three of us watched the moon rise over the mountains and listened to coyote songs. I missed the real Mary from Kansas and wished she were with me.

On a day when the aspen leaves jiggled on their stems in the wind, unwilling to part from their branches, I played at the edge of the river. I was alone and felt foolish for talking out loud to my doll. But why not? She was my only friend. I unscrewed Mary's hollow head. No one but me knew my secret treasures were kept inside. There was a hair ribbon from Mary, an earring that I found on the train, and a gold locket given to me by my grandmother.

Because of the noise of the rushing water over the rocks below, I never heard anyone coming. Suddenly, I saw a long shadow fall next to mine! I jumped up, and all my treasures spilled onto the rocks. For the first time in my life, I was face-to-face with a real Indian! I did not know what to say or do. Should I be afraid?

The shadow belonged to Lily. She looked like any other girl I knew, except her clothes and her skin were different. Hastily I grabbed my doll. Lily smiled and gathered up my treasures and held them out to me. I knew then not to be afraid.

In the beginning we giggled a lot, as it was not easy to learn each other's language. We used our hands to talk to each other. Lily showed me the Indian sign for flower.

She lived upriver, not far from us. Her family and the other Indians in her village lived in tepees built of wood poles and animal hides. At first when I visited Lily at her camp, everyone stared at me. Later, I helped to sew beads on moccasins and belts. Lily taught me the hoop-and-pole game.

Lily, however, was unusually quiet and shy when she visited our home. She was afraid of our cattle. They liked to come very close to us because they are such nosy beasts. We also picked ripe plums. Sometimes we threw them at each other and then we were not so quiet any more.

Lily had a doll, too, but it was not as fine as Mary. Lily´s doll was made of stuffed deer hide. It was only natural that she became more fond of my doll, and I guarded Mary a little jealously.

"I will give you a treasure to add to the inside of Mary's head," said Lily. The next time we met, she gave me a bracelet made of shells. I gave Lily chalk and a slate, and began to teach her how to read and write.

As the Indians would say, many moons passed overhead in the sky—two years' worth of moons to be exact. In the second year, during the Indian "Sturgeon" moon, or August, we had company. A wrangler from another ranch arrived and brought news with him.

"I heard soldiers are coming this way to round up the Indians," he said. I peered around the window from inside to hear more.

The wrangler continued talking when I joined Ma and Pa outside on the porch. "The Nez Perce Indians are living and grazing their horses on land that belongs to the miners and ranchers."

"Where are they going?" I asked fearfully.

"The army is going to move them to a reservation far from the river. I've heard fighting has already begun with one of the tribes. They don't want to go. They still think this is their land."

I spoke up in defense of my best friend, saying, "But Lily says the land has belonged to her people forever."

We had no time to discuss what could happen to Lily. The saddlebag doctor arrived as the wrangler was leaving. The doctor visited the families that lived up and down the river. He always managed to find a piece of candy for me among the pills and tonics he carried in his saddlebags.

While Pa and the doctor talked together, I said to Ma, "I'm afraid for Lily. I don't want the soldiers to take her away. I have to warn her!"

"Well, it would be too dangerous to go and see her," Ma answered. "And we can't send the Indians a message because they cannot read English."

My face brightened. "Oh yes we can send a message! Lily can read."

Then Ma and I came up with a plan. Slowly, in my best hand-writing, I wrote a note warning Lily and the other Indians that the soldiers were coming to take them away. We unscrewed Mary's head and put the note inside with all my treasures except one. I kept the bracelet so that I had a reminder of Lily.

After screwing the head back on, I asked the saddlebag doctor, "Will you please give this doll to my best friend, Lily, when you visit the Indian village? Black Eagle is her father." The doctor rode off with the doll peering out of his saddlebag.

Inside the cabin, I told Pa what I did. "Dr. MacDonald might not want to go there if he thought there could be trouble," I worried. "I put a note inside my doll's head. It's our secret hiding place. Lily would know to look inside and find my message." Pa agreed it was the right thing to do.

I never saw Lily again. I had never been filled with so much sorrow. We did not know what happened to Lily, as we heard the Indians had disappeared before the soldiers arrived. I knew that my doll had helped the Indians. What's more, I had given Lily a keepsake to comfort her when she left the canyon, just as Aunt Sophie had done for me.

Many more moons passed before my own family moved from the river. Now we live in a town a long day's journey from Salmon Creek. Each summer we come back to my parents' cabin. Wild sunflowers grow where our cattle used to graze. The plum trees droop because no one picks their fruit.

Upon our arrival this summer, our excitement turned to dismay. The front door had been left open. Anxiously, we peered in, not knowing what to expect. Sitting on a chair was my old doll, Mary! Although her dress was tattered and she was not so beautiful anymore, I was overjoyed to see her again. Slowly I began to unscrew the doll's head. Somehow I knew among all my old treasures, there would be a note. And there was:

To my best friend, Charlotte. I am at last able to return your doll. She has been well loved, but she belongs to you. My family and I have you to thank for the freedom we enjoy to this day. When you read this we will be far apart, but you will be forever in my heart.

Love, Lily

For the first time in my life, I understood how deep the roots of friendship could grow. Lily would be forever in my heart, too.

Author's Note

Best Friends is an invented story that takes place in the Snake River valley of the 1870s. Snake River country spreads over Idaho and eastern Oregon. It contains steep mountains, canyons, prairies, and forests. Among the lofty peaks, daily temperatures vary between extremes of heat and cold.

Despite the harsh climate along the river, people have lived for thousands of years in the valleys of the Snake and Clearwater Rivers in Idaho and in Oregon's Wallowa Mountains on the western shores of the Snake River. The Nez Perce Indians lived in these valleys before the white settlers came. Their tribe consisted of

many villages and smaller groups called bands. Each village had its own leaders. Their territory covered 10,000 square miles. A peaceful people, they lived on the abundant wildlife and vegetation of their territory.

The Homestead Act of 1862 opened up the land to white settlers. Each head of household was given 160 acres of surveyed land. After five years of residence and improvements, the homesteader gained title to the land. Creek and river access provided water for the settlers and their gardens and stock, as well as ample fish and game. Any provisions came over treacherous mountain passes or by river through swift currents and rapids. Despite the odds, many settlers like Charlotte's family lived successfully on cattle or sheep ranches. Others mined the mountains for copper, gold, silver, and other minerals.

Prior to the Homestead Act, the invasion of white settlers into the area led to a treaty in 1855 between the Nez Perce Indians and the United States Government. The treaty called for the creation of a reservation for the Indians. Some of the villages were divided about signing this treaty. The discovery of gold on Indian land resulted in another treaty in 1863, and the government took even more tribal land away from the Indians. Only the Chief Joseph band, living in Wallowa, Oregon, refused to move to the Idaho reservation. A great and bitter war followed. The Nez Perce attempted to flee and find peace in Montana. Forty-two miles from the Canadian border, with heavy losses to both sides, Chief Joseph surrendered in 1877.

The surviving Nez Perce were first banished to Oklahoma. Later, the Chief Joseph band survivors were settled on the Colville Indian Reservation in north-eastern Washington. Today, the Nez Perce National Historical Park commemorates these events and the history of the Nez Perce with sites throughout north-central Idaho, Oregon, Washington, and Montana.

Although the story of Charlotte and Lily is not a real story, I imagined that it took place during these troubled times. Lily could have been a member of the Chief Joseph band of Nez Perce Indians, and Charlotte could have been a rancher's daughter who empathized with the plight of the Indian. All of the artifacts shown in the book are things from the late 1800s that Charlotte and Lily might have seen, used, and played with.

—Loretta Krupinski

For *my* best friend, Bill
—L. K.

Grateful acknowledgement is made to Bob Chenoweth of the
Nez Perce National Historical Park for his help with this book.

The author would like to thank the following for permission to use the photographs in this book: Bob Chenoweth of the
Nez Perce National Historical Park: pages 3 (right), 13, 14, 18, 20, 28; Esther Hobbs: page 8; The Lyme Historical Society:
pages 3 (left), 5, 31, 32; Jane Rohling of Hell's Canyon National Recreation Area: pages 24 and 30; Weed Department,
University of Idaho: page 26. All other photos are from the author's personal collection.

Printed in Hong Kong by South China

First Edition
1 3 5 7 9 10 8 6 4 2

The artwork for each picture is prepared using gouache paints on Lanaguarelle watercolor paper.

This book is set in 18-point Locarno Light.

Library of Congress Cataloging-in-Publication Data

Krupinski, Loretta.
Best friends / Loretta Krupinski. — 1st ed.
p.   cm.
Summary: When a settler's young daughter learns that soldiers will force the Nez Perce off the nearby land,
she uses a doll to warn her Indian friend of the impending danger.
ISBN 0-7868-0332-0 (trade).—ISBN 0-7868-2356-9 (lib. bdg.).
[1. Best friends—Fiction. 2. Dolls—Fiction. 3. Nez Perce Indians—Fiction. 4. Indians of North America—Fiction.]
I. Title.
PZ7.K94624Be   1998
[E]—DC21   97-13102